MW00808182

ARASH **AMEL** MARGUERITE **BENNETT**

BUTTERFLY™

ANTONIO **FUSO** STEFANO **SIMEONE** ADAM **GUZOWSKI**

Published by
ARCHAIA™

“BEFORE HE PASSED, MY FATHER
TAUGHT ME TO SHOOT.”

BOOM! Studios, 5670 Wilshire Boulevard, Suite 450, Los Angeles, CA 90036-5679. Printed in China. First Printing.

ISBN: 978-1-60886-724-0, eISBN: 978-1-61398-395-9

CREATED & STORY BY
ARASH **AMEL**

WRITTEN BY
MARGUERITE **BENNETT**

ILLUSTRATED BY
ANTONIO **FUSO**
(CHAPTERS 1 - 2)
STEFANO **SIMEONE**
(CHAPTERS 3 - 4)

COLORED BY
ADAM **GUZOWSKI**

LETTERED BY
STEVE **WANDS**

COVER & COLLECTION DESIGN BY
SCOTT **NEWMAN**

ASSISTANT EDITOR
CAMERON **CHITTOCK**

EDITOR
REBECCA **TAYLOR**

SPECIAL THANKS TO
CORY **HOLMES**

CHAPTER **ONE**

WINCHESTER, VIRGINIA. 1988.
THE WAIT.

THE AIM.

CRKKKK!

BEFORE HE PASSED, MY FATHER TAUGHT ME TO SHOOT.

HE'D DIE GAGGING ON HIS OWN BLOOD FIVE YEARS LATER, SOMEWHERE IN THE SOMALI DESERT.

I DON'T KNOW IF THIS
MEMORY IS REAL.

MEMORY IS SO DELICATE,
LIKE THE REST OF US.

THE LITTLE
THINGS KILL US,
IN THE END.

THE KERNEL
OF PLAQUE IN
THE AORTA.

THE BEAD OF
BLOOD IN THE
FISSURE OF
THE BRAIN.

THE TIP OF A
BRASS COATED .22
ROUND AT 890 MPH.

OSLO, NORWAY. TODAY.
THIS CHEAP WINE IS WHAT MY FATHER DRANK, AND DRANK TOO MUCH OF, WHEN HE LIVED.
MY NAME WAS BECKY, THEN.
AND IN THE CIA, MY NAME WAS REBECCA FAULKNER.
BUT IN THE PROJECT, WE DON'T HAVE NAMES.
THOUGH SOMETIMES...
...THEY'LL CALL ME BUTTERFLY.

I AM A SET OF SKILLS, TO THE PROJECT.

beauty

DISGUISE.

HAND OFF.

COVER.
EXIT

GRAND HOTEL

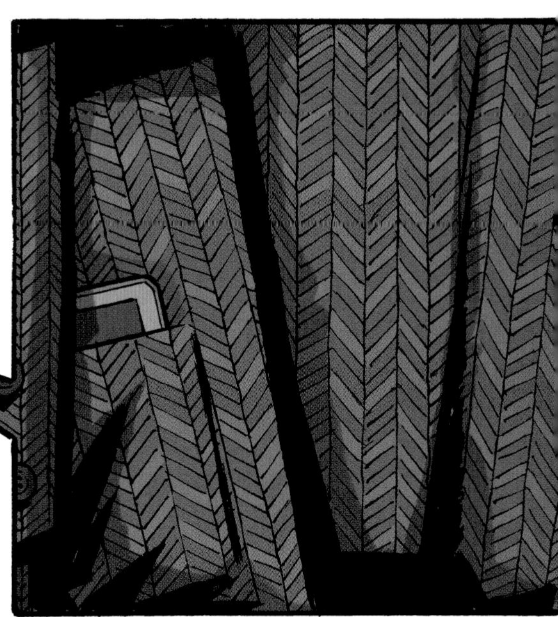

RETRIEVAL.

HGK
NO.
NO, NO, NO--
RETRIEVAL ONLY, NO LOSS OF LIFE--
SHELTER. NOW.

I WOULD LIKE A ROOM FOR THE EVENING, PLEASE. SINGLE BED.
AT ONCE, MISS.

TRIIIG! TRIIIIG! TRIIIIG!
THANK YOU--OH!
NOTHING TO WORRY YOU, MISS. THE ALARM IS LIKELY JUST A DRILL.

ОН УМЕР.

KLANG

ESCAPE.

THERE ARE THREE NUMBERS, FOR AGENTS IN THE FIELD.
ZZZT THIS NUMBER IS NO LONGER IN SERVICE. IF YOU HAVE REACHED THIS NUMBER IN ERROR--
PROTOCOL. HUXLEY, MY HANDLER.

LOGISTICS. MORTIMER, MY QUARTERMASTER.
ZZZT THIS NUMBER IS NO LONGER IN SERVICE. IF YOU--

AND A THIRD NUMBER I PRAY I DO NOT NEED.
216

KVA HEITER DU?
ANATOMY. INFANT NECKS ARE DELICATE.

KAN EG HJELPE DEG?

KAN DU HJELPE MEG?

BLI MED MEG...

GOODBYE, LITTLE ONE. THEY WON'T HURT YOU.
KVA HEITER DU?

353

-PING

INFILTRATION.

-PING

ANATOMY.
-SHUK

EVERY STOP, I WAIT FOR IT.
T·bane

THE STORM OF MERCENARIES.
THE POLICE.
THE BARRAGE OF GUNFIRE.

BUT AT EACH STOP--

THERE IS NOTHING.

WHY HAS NO ONE COME FOR ME?
THAT RUSSIAN OLIGARCH DROPPING DEAD, AT THE PRECISE MOMENT I WAS THERE ON RETRIEVAL... NO. THE PROJECT WOULDN'T DARE.
THERE ARE THREE NUMBERS.
ONE AND TWO ARE DEAD...

AND I HAVE NEVER USED THREE...
...UNTIL NOW.
CRRRK NIGHTINGALE. CRRRK 49.6117 DEGREES NORTH, 6.1300 EAST. CLIK

FERRY TO KIEL, GERMANY.
IN THE MORNING, THE NUMBERS ARE STILL DEAD.
NECESSARY TACTICS, MAYBE. A HORRIBLE COINCIDENCE.
MIKHAIL ILCHENKO CHOKED, AND I ONLY HAPPENED TO BE THERE...

KIEL HARBOR, GERMANY.
"NIGHTINGALE," THE MESSAGE SAID.
BUT NIGHTINGALE IS A MYTH TO TRAINEES AT THE PROJECT-- A BURNED OPERATIVE, A BOOGEYMAN, A CAUTIONARY TALE.

THE COORDINATES LEAD ME TO A SHIPYARD THAT HAD BEEN ABANDONED IN THE FIRST DAYS OF THE EUROPEAN UNION.

ABANDONED...
ALMOST.

WHY NIGHTINGALE? WHY THIS PLACE? THE PROJECT WOULD NEVER BURN ME. BUT AM I BECOMING NIGHTINGALE? IS THAT WHAT THIS MEANS?
SKREEEEE

I'VE FAILED, BECOME THE STORY THE NEW RECRUITS WILL WHISPER TO EACH OTHER IN THE DARK?

SOMEONE WAS HERE, BEFORE ME.

WHO WERE YOU?

YOU WAITED HERE, MAYBE, WHEN YOU WERE IN DANGER.
Le Papillon Rose

WERE YOU EVER RESCUED?

IT TOOK ME FOUR DAYS AND TWO DOZEN REDIALS TO UNDERSTAND THAT HELP WAS NOT COMING.
Le Papillon Rose

THE ENTIRE CRATE WAS PICKED OVER...
THIS BOTTLE CAN'T BE A COINCIDENCE.
Le Papillon Rose
1983

THE PROJECT WOULD NEVER BETRAY ME.
"A MEMORIAL SERVICE IN MOSCOW FOR CEO MIKHAIL ILCHENKO--"
"--DIED WHILE ON HOLIDAY IN OSLO--"
PEOPLE SEE WHAT THEY WANT TO SEE.

"--AUTHORITIES STILL SEARCHING FOR A WOMAN--"
"--EARNED HIS FORTUNE IN THE OIL INDUSTRY--"
A BRITISH STUDENT, BACKPACKING THROUGH THE WINTER HOLIDAY.

"--BELIEVED TO HAVE BEEN INVOLVED WITH MR. ILCHENKO'S DEATH--"

"--MOURNED AS A PHILANTHROPIST, THE FOUNDER OF SEVERAL CHARITIES--"
MEMORY IS SO DELICATE.

LE PAPILLION ROSE VINEYARD, BEAUJOLAIS, FRANCE. NOW.
LIKE THE REST OF US.
"CRRXX WE'VE GOT HER. CLIK"

THERE'S A CATCH. THERE MUST BE A CATCH.

MARTIN! LE DINER EST PRÊT!

CRRRK NIGHTINGALE. CRRRK 47.6117 DEGREES NORTH, 6.1300 EAST. CLIK

A TRAP?

THE WAIT.
THE AIM.

THE EXPLOSION.
...DAD?
AS LONG AS I'M ALIVE.

TEN MINUTES AGO, MY DAUGHTER WAS HIKING IN THE ALPS.
AND I? I WAS HERE, WITH MY FAMILY.
AND YOU THOUGHT YOU WERE TOO OLD TO BE A FATHER, DAVID.
MARTIN! SUPPER IS READY!
BE THERE IN A MOMENT, ANGELIQUE...
WAS IT A TRAP?
THEY WERE MOVING QUIETLY UP AHEAD, THE FOOTSTEPS OF SOMEONE TRAINED TO BE DISCREET...
IF IT WERE AN ENEMY, THAT CLOSE TO MY HOME, THAT CLOSE TO MY FAMILY, MY WIFE, MY SON--
EVERYTHING THAT CAME BEFORE WILL HAVE BEEN FOR NOTHING.

ONE YEAR AGO.
EVERY YEAR SINCE I HAVE COME TO FRANCE, I HAVE WORKED TO PROTECT MY FAMILY.
I HAVE WORKED FOR BRIDGEWELL LTD.
FIVE YEARS AGO, I WAS REMINDED OF THE PROTECTION FAMILIES NEED.
WE HAD A BOY. MARTIN. WE WENT ON A DAY TRIP TO PARIS, WITH LEO, HIS GODFATHER.
A MAN IN THE STREET THOUGHT HE KNEW ME.
A MAN IN THE STREET DIDN'T GO HOME.

EIGHT YEARS AGO, I MET A WOMAN IN BEAUJOLAIS. SHE WORE HONEYSUCKLE IN HER HAIR...
HER FAMILY'S VINEYARD WAS FAILING. A LOCAL THUG WANTED THE LAND.
I TOOK CARE OF IT--
--AND OF HER.

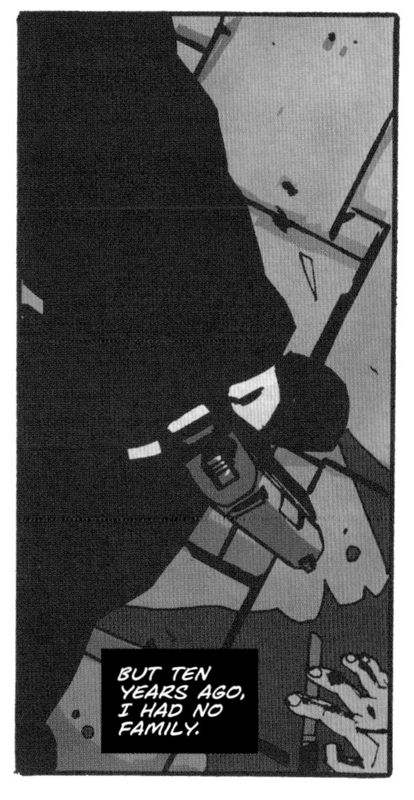
BUT TEN YEARS AGO, I HAD NO FAMILY.

JUNE, 2004.
I BEGAN WORKING FOR A COMPANY CALLED BRIDGEWELL LTD, WHICH SPECIALIZED IN PRIVATE CONTRACTING.
THEY KNEW ABOUT THE TIME I'D SPENT IN THE CIA. THEY KNEW ABOUT THE DEPARTMENT OF DEFENSE, TOO.
AND THEY KNEW ABOUT THE SPECIAL DIVISION I HAD MADE.
AT BRIDGEWELL LTD, PEOPLE CAME TO US...PEOPLE WITH PROBLEMS.
AND WE... HELPED.
WHEN I ASKED ABOUT OUR EMPLOYER, MY NEW ASSOCIATES LAUGHED, OR PALED, OR LOOKED AWAY.
RAVEN, THEY CALLED HIM, WHEN THEY CALLED HIM ANYTHING.
NO ONE COULD AGREE IF HE WAS ONE MAN OR TEN--LIVING, OR DEAD, OR A GHOST.
I'VE NEVER MET HIM.
THE HARBOR BOSS HAD SEEN ME HANDLE A THIEF WHO STOLE A SHIPMENT FROM A VERY...SIGNIFICANT MAN.
I WAS WORKING FREELANCE THEN.
HE WAS THE ONE WHO MADE INTRODUCTIONS.
WHO WAS I TO REFUSE?
TEN YEARS AGO, I DIDN'T HAVE A FAMILY.
TWENTY YEARS AGO, I DIDN'T EVEN HAVE A COUNTRY.

DECEMBER 21, 1993. SOMALIA.
012W
DEAD MEN SELDOM DO.
AND I WAS A DEAD MAN, AFTER ALL.
DEAD TO THE COUNTRY I SERVED.
A MAN HAS TO BE A PARTICULAR KIND OF LIAR, TO FAKE HIS OWN DEATH.
AND A PARTICULAR KIND OF MONSTER.
I'D BRIBED A LOCAL MILITANT TO FIRE ON OUR TRANSPORT.
I'D BRIBED ONE OF THE LOCAL GRAVEDIGGERS TO FIND ME ON THE FIELD.

I DEALT WITH THEM ALL THE SAME.

DECEMBER 14, 1993.
I COULD HEAR THE SCREAMS AND THE GUNFIRE A VILLAGE AWAY.
WE CAME HERE TO HELP PEOPLE.
THAT'S WHAT THE PENTAGON WANTED US TO BELIEVE.

THE THREAT HAD BEEN DELIVERED BY A FRIEND, BUT IT WAS DELIVERED ALL THE SAME.
I'D BEEN DISCOVERED.
MY WIFE... AND MY DAUGHTER...

REBECCA...
AS LONG AS I WAS ALIVE, MY FAMILY COULD BE PUNISHED AND TORTURED TO FIND ME.
AS LONG AS I WAS ALIVE.

CHAPTER **TWO**

LE PAPILLION ROSE VINEYARD, BEAUJOLAIS, FRANCE. NOW.
HOW DO YOU OUTRUN THE DEAD?
HOW DO YOU ESCAPE?

FRAGILE AND INJURED AND STUNNED--

--THE BUTTERFLY AGAINST THE BLAST OF ETHER.

...DAD?
MY FATHER.

WHY THE HELL WOULD YOU CALL ME THAT?
THE HERO.

WHO ARE YOU?!
MY FATHER...IS ALIVE. IT DOESN'T MAKE ANY...DAD--

BUTTERFLY. GIVEN NAME, REBECCA FAULKNER. PROJECT DELTA.
AND YOU'RE... YOU'RE NIGHTIN-GALE. THE LEGEND.
THE COORDINATES LED ME TO YOUR--

I DON'T HAVE A DAUGHTER. I NEVER DID.
YOUR NAME IS DAVID! DAVID FAULKNER!

IS THIS A TEST? ...SIR?
PAPA!

...PAPA?

TU PEUX M'AIDER...? SUIS-MOI...

BANG
MAMA!
DAVID?
WOUAFF! WOUAFF!

PAPA, QUI EST-CE?
WOUAFF! WOUAFF!

OH, NO.

OH, **FUCK** NO.

ANG... ANGLAIS, OUI?

DAVID?
WOUAAA--

SHE ISN'T WHO SHE SAYS SHE IS.
DAVID, JUST LOOK AT HER! SHE HAS MARTIN'S EYES.
ANGELIQUE! A WORD, PLEASE?
IT'S YOU...

SLAM
MARTIN?

DO YOU LIKE DINOSAURS?

I WAS TWELVE WHEN MEN IN BLACK SUITS CAME TO OUR HOUSE AND TOLD ME THAT MY FATHER WAS A HERO...
...AND THAT MY FATHER WAS DEAD.
THE WHOLE OF MY LIFE WAS SHADOWED BY THAT MEMORY...SWALLOWED UP BY THE LEGEND OF WHO AND WHAT MY FATHER WAS.
HIS **SACRIFICE**.
ALL THE WHILE, HE'S BEEN HIDING IN A FRENCH VINEYARD, PLAYING HUSBAND AND WIFE, DRINKING CHEAP WINE, AND FUCKING A WOMAN YOUNGER THAN I AM.
MY MOTHER WAS NEVER THE SAME AFTER MY FATHER DIED. SHE BECAME BITTER, SELFISH, FEARFUL.
SHE REMARRIED, I WENT OFF TO COLLEGE, AND JUST...DIDN'T COME BACK.
THE PROJECT RECRUITED ME NOT LONG AFTER GRADUATION.
WHEN THIS BOY WAS TAKING HIS FIRST STEPS, I ALREADY HAD A GUN IN MY HAND.
MARTIN. MY **BROTHER**.
I DIDN'T EVEN KNOW I--OH--
HE NAME-- AH, **COMMENT DIT-ON**...
HIS NAME IS PHILIPPE.

...REBECCA? I'M ANGELIQUE, DAVID'S WIFE.
YOU AND MARTIN SHOULD KNOW ONE ANOTHER. WE'D BE SO HAPPY IF YOU WOULD STAY WITH US, FOR AS LONG AS YOU LIKE.
I NEED TO GET BACK TO THE PROJECT.
I NEED TO GET BACK UNDER CONTROL.
YOUR FATHER PROTECTED ME WHEN THE BROKERS CAME FOR THE VINEYARD. THEN THE BEAUJOLAIS NOUVEAU BECAME SO POPULAR, AND...WELL.
IT ISN'T ELEGANT, PERHAPS, BUT IT GETS THE JOB DONE.
WOULD YOU LIKE A GLASS OF WINE? I KNOW THIS MUST BE OVER-WHELMING.
TWO ENTRANCES INTO THE HOUSE. DECENT VISIBILITY FROM THE WINDOWS.

I DON'T DRINK.
CHRIST.
I STILL HAVE THE AUTOMATIC. THE WOMAN AND BOY AREN'T A THREAT. IF I COULD MAKE IT TO THE WOODS--
MARTIN, PLEASE HELP ME WITH THE DISHES? OH, AND GRAB THAT TABLECLOTH, SOME STAINS DON'T COME OUT--
DAVID, REBECCA--WHY DON'T YOU TWO GO INTO THE STUDY?

"I'M SURE YOU HAVE SO MUCH TO SAY, AFTER TWENTY YEARS."

HOW DID YOU FIND ME?

Le Papillon

Le Papillon Rose
1983
WHEN I WAS A CHILD, MY FATHER, DAVID **FAULKNER**, HAD THIS ONE WINE... NOT EVEN A GOOD KIND.
THIS CHEAP, FRUITY STUFF--I NEVER KNEW WHY IT WAS SO...HE SAVED IT FOR SPECIAL OCCASIONS.

WHAT WERE YOU TOASTING, ON THAT **SPECIAL DAY?**
THE DAY YOU... WHAT? **FAKED YOUR DEATH?**

SO?
Beaujolais
Le Papillon Rose
1983
ALC. 12.5% BY VOL
750 ML

WHY ARE YOU BEING SO **CRUEL?**

IF YOU HAD ANY IDEA HOW MANY WOMEN AND CHILDREN...
BUT YOU'RE A CHILD.
I'M NO OLDER THAN YOUR WIFE, WHO IS FAR GENTLER AND MORE FORGIVING THAN YOU COULD EVER DESERVE.

TELL ME HOW YOU GOT HERE. TELL ME EVERYTHING.

MY PROJECT... OR MY **FATHER?**
WHAT COULD I GAIN BY TELLING HIM? TRUST? INFORMATION?
THE PROJECT HASN'T COME FOR ME...AND HE COULD BE THE KEY TO **WHY.**

--THEN WHEN I WAS ON THE HILL OVERLOOKING THE VINEYARD, I CALLED THE THIRD NUMBER AGAIN, THE ONE I'D NEVER TRIED BEFORE, FOR EXTRACTION--
NO...

GET UP. WE HAVE TO LEAVE, NOW--

YOU **AMATEUR.** YOU'VE LED THE PROJECT AND THE REST RIGHT TO US.
SO?

THE THIRD NUMBER SIGNALS THE PROJECT'S FLIGHT PROTOCOL. A SATELLITE LOCATION.

THEY'VE KNOWN WHERE YOU ARE THIS ENTIRE TIME AND CHOSEN NOT TO COME FOR YOU.
THEY WERE WAITING UNTIL YOU LED THEM TO SOMETHING THEY WANTED.

JUST LIKE THAT, I'M THE IDIOT CHILD AGAIN, WITH HIS HANDS AROUND MY HANDS AROUND THE TRIGGER OF MY FIRST RIFLE.
YOU'VE ALREADY BEEN HERE FORTY-FIVE MINUTES. WE HAVE LESS THAN FIFTEEN BEFORE PROJECT DELTA ARRIVES TO COLLECT YOU.
WE HAVE TO GET TO BRIDGE-WELL.

YOU'VE BEEN SET UP, LITTLE BUTTERFLY.
...BRIDGEWELL?
WHO THE FUCK IS BRIDGEWELL?

AND WHATEVER ELSE HAPPENS...I AM GOING TO KEEP MY FAMILY SAFE.
YOU DON'T NEED ME FOR THAT.
ALL OF MY FAMILY. YOU'RE LEAVING PROJECT DELTA BEHIND.
ANGELIQUE! MARTIN!
THOOM

DAVID? WHAT IS--?
ANGELIQUE, YOU NEED TO PACK IMMEDIATELY, ONLY WHAT YOU NEED--
THOOM
THOOM
FIVE MINUTES, AND THEN WE NEED TO BE IN THE CAR--
SKTCHSKTCHSKTCH

SKTCHSKTCHSKTCH

OOF
THEY'RE SCARED OF THE THUNDER--

THAT'S NOT THUNDER.

WHAT HAVE I DONE?

DECEMBER 13, 1993. SOMALIA.
HOW DO YOU OUTRUN THE DEAD? HOW DO YOU ESCAPE?
ITALY
INDIAN OCEAN

BARNEY TAYLOR, MY CASE OFFICER.
JUNO LUND. ANOTHER OPERATIVE, LIKE ME.
DAVID! WHY ARE YOU HIDING?
PE-YEW, BOY--WHAT'S THAT STINK? I KNOW IT ISN'T HOME, BUT BATHS--

AHH, THERE'S THE STINK. SMUGGLED IN, EH? NEVER COULD QUIT YOUR LIQUOR, COULD YOU--STILL GOT THAT BOTTLE OF BEAUJOLAIS I GAVE YOU?

OOF, BITTER! PAR FOR THE COURSE FOR YOU, THOUGH, ISN'T IT, HAHA?
...I'M AFRAID I DON'T FOLLOW, BARNEY.

AH. NO HARM MEANT. JUST, AH... THE CIA WAS NEVER HAPPY TO WATCH YOU LEAVE FOR THE DEPARTMENT OF DEFENSE, WAS IT?
THEY REALLY POACHED YOU FOR PROJECT DELTA THERE, BOY.

JUST... TREAD LIGHTLY, HUH? GOOD MAN.

ONE HOUR BEFORE.
WE WERE MEANT TO BRING PEACE TO THE REGION.
CLEAN WATER. SAFE SCHOOLS.

INSTEAD, WE WERE ROOTING OUT MILITANTS OPPOSED TO AN OIL PIPELINE--
--A PIPELINE THAT DID NOT APPEAR IN ANY KNOWN RECORD FOR THE DEPARTMENT OF DEFENSE OR THE CIA.
BUT MIRANDA...
I NEEDED TO GET A MESSAGE TO MIRANDA.

ONCE THE MILITANTS WERE EXTINGUISHED, I BELIEVED THE PIPELINE WOULD BE SOLD TO WHICHEVER CORPORATE INTEREST PROJECT DELTA CHOSE.

THEY WERE GOING TO KILL MY WIFE, AND THEY WERE GOING TO KILL MY DAUGHTER, REBECCA.
UNLESS I GOT WORD TO MIRANDA ABOUT THE OIL...
HOW MANY MORE WOMEN AND CHILDREN WOULD DIE?

TWO HOURS BEFORE.
FATIMA. SHE WAS A WASHERWOMAN-- ONE OF THE REFUGEES.
ALWAYS GOT THE STAINS OUT, DID SHE?
UGLY BUSINESS. I'M SORRY FOR THEIR LOSS. PRICE OF OUR WORK HERE.

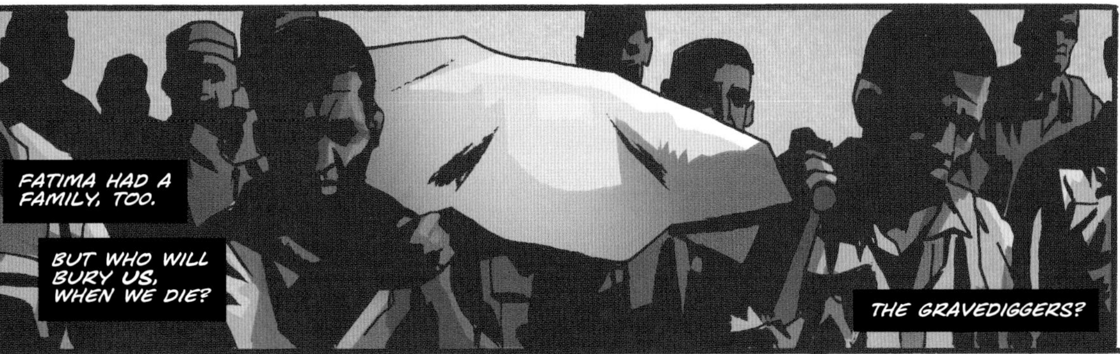
FATIMA HAD A FAMILY, TOO.
BUT WHO WILL BURY US, WHEN WE DIE?
THE GRAVEDIGGERS?

WHEN THEY DIE, THEY SAY THE SALAT AL-JANAZAH. BURY THE BODY TO FACE THE QIBLA.
WHEN WE DIE, THEY READ OUT WHO KILLED US FROM A MANILA ENVELOPE. ATTACH LABELS TO OUR TOES. BURN US TO A FINE, SHIMMERING SAND.

I READ THE REPORT ON HER DEATH--FATIMA.

THEY SAID SHE WAS KILLED BY SOMALI MILITANTS--MEN IN THE SERVICE OF THE WARLORD MUHAMMED AIDID.
BUT I KNEW BETTER.

THREE HOURS BEFORE.
CHRIST, THEY'VE BEEN WAILING OUTSIDE FOR HOURS! I THOUGHT IT WAS FORBIDDEN--
THEY'RE MOURNING THE DEATH OF THAT WOMAN--TELLING THE STORY OF HER LIFE.
TELLING TALES GETS YOU IN TROUBLE IN THIS WORLD. YOU KNOW THAT.

DAVID... DAVID, PLEASE. YOU KNOW WHAT I'M TALKING ABOUT.
STOP RECORDING WHAT THE PROJECT'S BEEN DOING. THIS IS PENTAGON.
I DON'T WANT TO BE THE ONE TO SAY IT, DAVID, BUT YOU HAVE TO LISTEN TO SOMEONE.
WHAT WE DID IN MOGADISHU--

--NEEDED TO BE DONE. AND THAT POOR BOY IN THE DESERT...BUT THE STORY WE TOLD IS THE TRUTH. NEEDS TO BE THE TRUTH.
THINK OF THE MORALE OF THOSE TWENTY-TWO-YEAR-OLD JARHEADS! THE BLACK HAWK FIASCO...
NOBODY NEEDS TO KNOW.

YOU CAN'T RUN FROM WHO YOU ARE, DAVID...
YOU CAN'T CHANGE WHO YOU ARE.

I'M GOING TO PAY MY RESPECTS.

THE MOHEET HOTEL, MOGADISHU, SOMALIA. NOVEMBER 29, 1993.
JUNO...
DAVID. DAVID, GET UP...
WE'VE BEEN COMPRO-MISED.

HOTEL SAHAFI
TERNATIONAL
RECEPION
TWENTY-SEVEN DEATHS IN THE HOTEL THAT DAY.
FIVE OF AIDID'S MILITANTS WERE KILLED. SIX CIVILIAN MEN.
BUT THE REST WERE WOMEN AND CHILDREN.
BAWOOOOM

THE MOHEET HOTEL, MOGADISHU, SOMALIA. NOVEMBER 28, 1993.
WE HAD INFORMATION THAT AIDID'S MEN WERE USING THE BACK ROOMS OF THE MOHEET HOTEL AS A HEADQUARTERS.
THESE WERE MEN RESPONSIBLE FOR MASSACRES, RAPES, THE BAYONETING OF CHILDREN.

JUNO AND I WERE SENT TO ROOT THEM OUT.
PLAY HUSBAND AND WIFE.

OUR TARGETS...

...AND THEIR HUMAN SHIELDS.

YOU CAN STILL KILL THEM WHEN YOU'RE DONE FUCKING ME.

Stairs down

WE CAN'T GO THROUGH WITH THIS--WE HAVE TO GO BACK TO BASE--
ARE YOU CRAZY, DAVID?! THIS IS OUR ONLY CHANCE BEFORE THEY REALIZE--
WE NEED MORE OPERATIVES--WE CAN TAKE THEM IN THEIR BEDS--

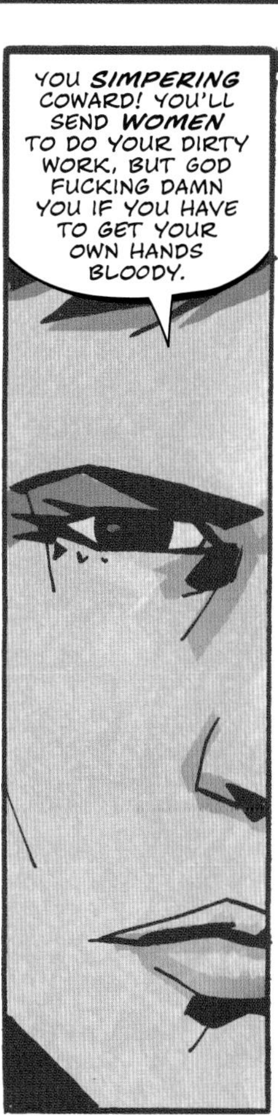
YOU *SIMPERING* COWARD! YOU'LL SEND *WOMEN* TO DO YOUR DIRTY WORK, BUT GOD FUCKING DAMN YOU IF YOU HAVE TO GET YOUR OWN HANDS BLOODY.

WHAT DO YOU THINK I AM?

LOYAL.
DON'T YOU DARE PROVE ME WRONG.

OUTSIDE OF THE PROJECT DELTA BASE. NOVEMBER 14, 1993.
SO, MUCH TO WASH TODAY, FATIMA? THE BOYS STAIN THE TABLE-CLOTHS?
I'M AFRAID THESE ARE FUNERAL SHROUDS, MR. FAULKNER.

FATIMA... DO YOU TRUST ME?

IF SOMEONE NEEDED TO LEAVE THE COUNTRY--AS A REFUGEE, MAYBE--WHERE WOULD HE OR SHE TURN?
THAT... ISN'T A VERY SAFE QUESTION, MR. FAULKNER.
BUT... FOR YOUR SAKE...I WILL INQUIRE.

PROJECT DELTA CAMP.
NOVEMBER 13, 1993.
AHHH, NOW *THAT* WAS A MEAL. WHAT A HELL, TO BE ENLISTED!
BLOOD AND OIL.

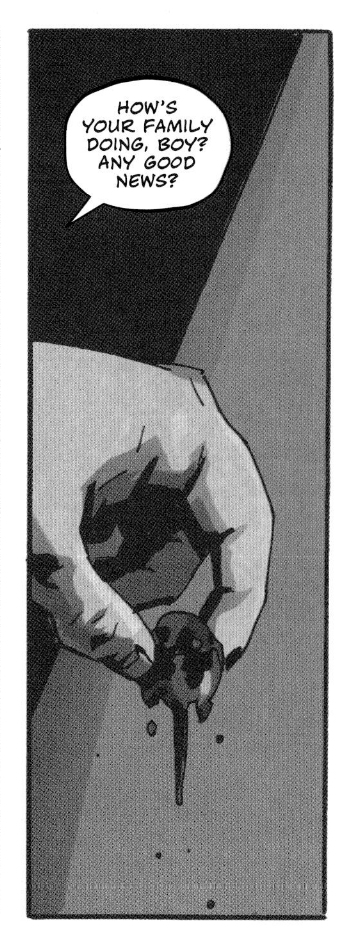
HOW'S YOUR FAMILY DOING, BOY? ANY GOOD NEWS?

THEY DO ALL RIGHT WITHOUT YOU THERE? THOSE LONG ABSENCES OF YOURS.

THIS IS NICE, ISN'T IT.
GOD, SO MUCH BETTER THAN BEING IN ALL THAT MUD AND CHAOS OUT THERE. BETTER FOOD, BETTER SERVICE.
TABLECLOTHS ON THE TABLES THAT *FATIMA* KEEPS SO CLEAN...

THESE LITTLE REMINDERS--
--OF HOME.

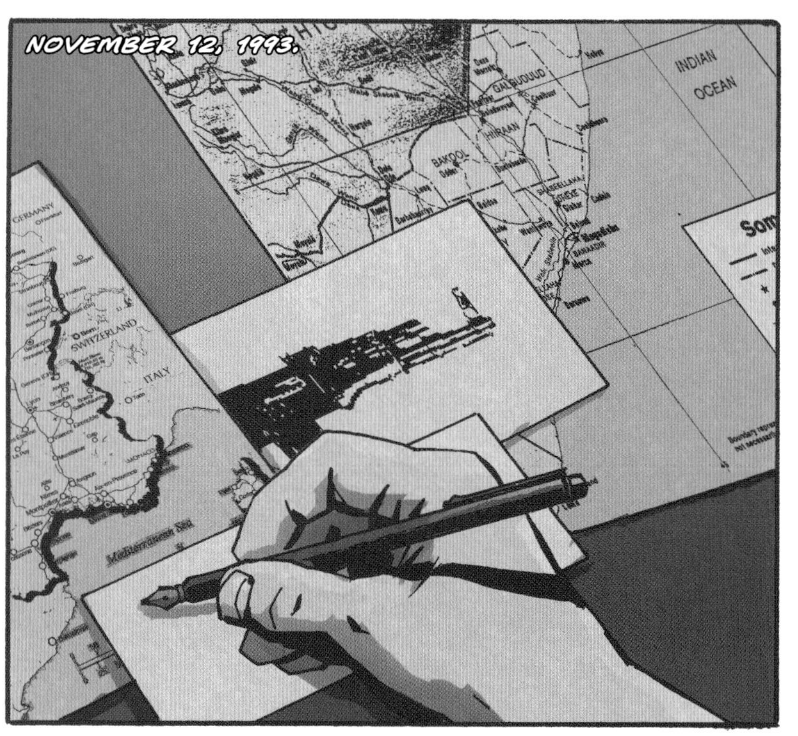
NOVEMBER 12, 1993.
INDIAN
OCEAN
SWITZERLAND
ITALY

THE LITTLE THINGS KILL US, IN THE END.
ITALY

THE RISK, THE COST...
ITALY

I'D THOUGHT I WAS SO CAREFUL.
ONLY PEN AND PAPER, ONLY SCRIBBLES, SKETCHES...
BUT INK SOAKS, LIKE BLOOD.
AND CLOTH REMEMBERS, LIKE FLESH.

AND ALL FOR ONE RUINED TABLECLOTH...
...I LEARNED I WAS WRONG.
MIRANDA

CHAPTER **THREE**

LE PAPILLION ROSE VINEYARD, BEAUJOLAIS, FRANCE. NOW.
EXCEPT FOR THE DUFFLE BAGS OF SEMI-AUTOMATICS AND THE CLAUSTROPHOBIC SENSE OF DOOM, THIS COULD BE A FAMILY OUTING.
MY FATHER, WHO FAKED HIS DEATH IN SOMALIA TWENTY YEARS AGO.
MY NEW STEPMOTHER, WHO IS YOUNGER THAN I AM.
AND MY LITTLE BROTHER, WHO I DIDN'T KNOW EXISTED UNTIL AN HOUR AGO.

AND ME...THE DISGRACED EX-AGENT OF PROJECT DELTA, WHO--IF MY ESTRANGED FATHER IS TO BE BELIEVED--LED OUR ENEMIES STRAIGHT TO HIS FRONT DOOR.
WHEN WILL WE COME HOME?

THE FARM OF LEO TRAVERE. TWENTY-ONE MINUTES LATER.
LEO, CHRIST--
IT'S ALL RIGHT, DAVID, GOT YOUR MESSAGE. YOU CALLED BRIDGEWELL YET?

THIS ISN'T BRIDGEWELL'S AFFAIR, LEO. I NEED YOU TO TAKE MY WIFE AND SON TO PARIS IMMEDIATELY.
I HAVE CASH, WEAPONS, PASSPORTS-- WHATEVER YOU'LL NEED TO STAY HIDDEN FOR THE TIME BEING.

WE'LL TALK SOON, REBECCA. IT WAS A JOY TO MEET YOU.

HOW'S MY FAVORITE GODSON?
HENRIETTA HAD A FOAL YESTERDAY! WANT TO TAKE YOUR MAMA BACK TO THE BARN TO SEE THEM?

IT'S ALL RIGHT, DAVID. I WON'T LET ANYTHING COME AGAINST YOUR FAMILY, FRAGILE THINGS THEY ARE. I STILL REMEMBER THAT SUMMER--WOULDN'T BE STANDING HERE IF NOT FOR YOU.
GOD, THAT GIRL COULD SHOOT.
SAY GOODBYE TO YOUR WOMAN AND BOY. YOU GOT A LONG ROAD TO TRAVEL.

DO YOU KNOW HOW MUCH I'LL MISS YOU?

AT DUSK, WHEN THE SHADOWS GROW SO LONG...

ANGELIQUE... ANGELIQUE, NO...
KEEP IT. AND COME FIND US.
COME FIND ME.

PAPA?

REVIENS, ET NOUS POUVONS FAIRE ENCORE DES ANGES DANS LA NEIGE.

REVIENS...
"COME BACK."

N ROUTE.
I WANT TO GO BACK.
I WANT TO GO BACK TO PROJECT DELTA.
THE PAST TWO HOURS HAVE BEEN...INSANITY.
I NEED TO GET BACK TO MY HOME.
WHAT'S OUR DESTINATION?
PARIS BUT FIRST WE'LL DRAW THEIR FIRE. KEEP THEM AWAY FROM MY FAMILY.
WE'LL BE SAFE IN THE CITY, IF ONLY FOR A LITTLE WHILE.
I'VE GIVEN IT SOME THOUGHT, AND I THINK MIKHAIL ILCHENKO WAS POISONED HOURS BEFORE I EVER SET FOOT IN THE HOTEL. I--
I DON'T THINK ILCHENKO WAS PARTICULAR. HIS DEATH SERVED A PURPOSE--PUTTING YOU TO FLIGHT. COULD'VE BEEN CIA, OR THE PENTAGON, OR THE PROJECT.
I THINK YOU WERE SET UP IN ORDER TO FIND ME. STARTLE ME OUT OF HIDING.
THEY COULD'VE KNOWN HE WAS SICK, SENT YOU ANYWAY. COULD'VE POISONED HIM THEMSELVES, TO MAKE YOU PANIC. THEY NEEDED YOU SCARED.
I MAY HAVE BROUGHT THE ENEMIES...BUT THEY WERE MY FATHER'S, IN THE END.
THE FAMILY, THE SECRETS, THE ANSWERS...EVERYTHING WAS ALWAYS MY FATHER'S, IN THE END.

AND I AM SICK TO DEATH OF HIM AND HIS LIES AND HIS GAMES.
BEFORE HE PASSED, MY FATHER TAUGHT ME TO SHOOT.
THE HERO. THE HYPOCRITE.

WAIT, SOMETHING'S WRONG. THERE SHOULD BE--
WHAT DO YOU NOTICE?

NO TRAFFIC. THERE WERE OTHER CARS BEFORE.
IT'S A TRAP.
ROADBLOCK, IS MY GUESS. MAYBE A CHECKPOINT. AGENTS WHO PROBABLY CAME IN ON THE CHOPPER.

TAKE ONE.
...
WHY THE HESITATION? NEVER USED ONE BEFORE?

SOMETIMES I HAVE DREAMS ABOUT A DAY YOU TOOK ME SHOOTING.

TWO KILOMETERS NORTH.
SOMETIMES I HAVE DREAMS.

ABOUT THE BOTTLES ON THE FENCE RAIL.

ABOUT THE GREEN-GOLD OF THE SUNSET THROUGH THE TREES.

ZZZT-- UN QUATRE-QUATRE ABANDONNE-- ZZZT--AU BORD DE LA ROUTE--A DEUX KILOMETERS-- ZZZT

AND THE WIND IN THE VIRGINIA PINES.

I HAVE DREAMS ABOUT THE WEIGHT OF THE GUN

STEADIED BY YOUR HANDS.

ABOUT THE EXPLOSIONS OF RED GLASS.

LIKE WINE, LIKE BLOOD.

ABOUT YOUR EYES.

WHICH ARE MY EYES.
AND SOMEONE ELSE'S EYES, NOW, TOO.

I HAVE DREAMS ABOUT HOW YOU ARE IN EVERY PART
OF EVERYTHING I HAVE
CRK!
OR AM
LÀ!
OR HAVE EVER DONE.
DREAMS ABOUT THE MAN I NOW WISH
CRK!
CRKCRKCRK
CRK!
CRK!
HAD NEVER COME BACK
FROM HIS OWN PRIVATE WAR.
CRK!
CRK!

IT'S NOT THAT MUCH DIFFERENT FROM TARGET SHOOTING, IS IT, DAD?
NO. NOT BY MUCH.

AGH!

CRK!
CRK!

GET-- CAR-- STAUNCH--!

GET IT YOURSELF.

BECKY!
DON'T YOU DARE USE HER NAME.
TWENTY YEARS, YOU LEFT ME.
DON'T YOU FUCKING DARE USE YOUR DAUGHTER'S NAME.

YOU'RE A LIAR. THE PROJECT WOULD NEVER LEAVE ME TO DIE.
BUT THAT'S EXACTLY WHAT'S ABOUT TO HAPPEN TO YOU.

YOU COULD'VE DIED THE HERO.

YOU SHOULD'VE DIED THE HERO.

I DID IT. I LEFT MY FATHER... NIGHTINGALE BEHIND.
AS EASILY AS HE EVER LEFT ME BEHIND.

I CALL THE THIRD NUMBER ONE LAST TIME.
AND AT LAST...
SOMEONE ANSWERS.

PROCEED... 1800 METERS... NORTH BY NORTHWEST... FOR... RETRIEVAL.

I KNOW NOW I WAS RIGHT. I MADE THE RIGHT CHOICE.
ESCAPE. EXTRACTION.

PROTOCOL.
YOU MADE IT.

FIRST.
LAST.
DOG.
DRINK.
LONDON.
OSLO.
CERBERUS.
DRINK...IS OLD CODE. COMPROMISED CODE.

NO...
NOT MY PROJECT, TOO.
CLIK

NO...
PLEASE, NO...
NOT AGAIN.

OH, THE SHADOWS GROW SO LONG.

INTERPOL, THE RUSSIANS, THE PROJECT...
PARIS, HE SAID. NIGHTINGALE WAS GOING TO FIND HIS FAMILY AGAIN IN PARIS.
NIGHTINGALE WAS RIGHT.
THE PROJECT BETRAYED ME. ANYONE COULD BE AN ENEMY.
AND THE ONLY PERSON I COULD'VE TRUSTED...
I LEFT IN THE SNOW TO DIE.
HOW FUCKED AM I?

NOVEMBER 10, 1993.
SOMALIA.
WE WERE SUPPOSED TO BE THE GOOD GUYS.

I WAS BEING WATCHED.
I DIDN'T KNOW IF IT WAS JUNO OR BARNEY OR FATIMA OR ALL THREE--
--I'D RECORDED EVERYTHING PROJECT DELTA HAD DONE IN SOMALIA, OFF THE RECORD.

INCLUDING THAT.

MY WIFE GAVE ME THE PEN FOR OUR ANNIVERSARY.
I NEEDED TO GO HOME.
MIRAND

SOMETHING TERRIBLE HAPPENED THE DAY BEFORE.

ONE DAY BEFORE.
GUNS, BARNEY! AIDID'S MEN HAVE RUSSIAN MILITARY-ISSUE ASSAULT RIFLES--
WHY WOULD THE RUSSIANS SEND GUNS HERE?
THE ANSWER, OF COURSE, WAS THAT THE RUSSIANS WERE GOING TO BENEFIT FROM PROJECT DELTA'S SUCCESS. BUT I WAS TOO NAIVE TO SEE THAT, YET.
WHY WOULDN'T THE RUSSIANS FUND OUR ENEMIES, IF THEY SUSPECTED AMERICANS IN THE REGION?
THE REAL QUESTION IS WHY HERE, WHY NOW, WHY THE EXPENSE?

AFRICA'S DROWNING IN RUSSIAN GUNS, JUNO. BLACK MARKET, SMUGGLERS, PIRATES--ALL THE UNDERWORLD WE'VE BEEN ROUNDING UP--IT DOESN'T PROVE ANYTHING.
THESE AREN'T JUST BOOTLEG AK-47S YOU FIND ON THE STREETS OF MOMBASA, BARNEY.
THESE ARE TOP OF THE LINE SR-3 VIKHR RIFLES, STRAIGHT OFF THE ASSEMBLY LINE AT THE TULA ARMS PLANT IN RUSSIA...
SOMEBODY IN THE KREMLIN IS DETERMINED WE DON'T FINISH A SIMPLE RELIEF JOB HERE. I WANT TO KNOW WHY.

AHHH, DAVID, THE RUSSIANS HATE SEEING ANYBODY DOING WELL ANYWHERE! EVEN THE SOMALIANS, ESPECIALLY IF WE'RE HELPING THEM.
ARE WE MAKING MOVES INTO SOMALIA? DO WE WANT TO REPLACE AIDID WITH OUR OWN GUY? IS THIS A COUP DISGUISED AS HUMANITARIAN AID?
WHAT WE ARE DOING IN SOMALIA IS AN EXAMPLE OF PROJECT DELTA IN ACTION. IF WE ARE POISONING THESE PEOPLE AGAINST AMERICAN INTERESTS--
TELL ME NOW, BARNEY. DO NOT FUCK WITH ME.
IT'S JUST RELIEF WORK, DAVID.

ONE HOUR BEFORE.
"GOD'S TRUTH."
FATIMA! HAVE YOU SEEN BARNEY TAYLOR? HE ISN'T IN HIS TENT.
GOOD AFTERNOON, JUNO. NO, I BELIEVE HE'LL BE BACK SOON.

WHERE DID YOU LEARN ENGLISH, FATIMA?
I WENT TO SCHOOL, SAME AS YOU I SUPPOSE, JUNO.
WHAT DID YOU WANT TO LEARN IT FOR?
IT WAS ONE OF THE LANGUAGES THAT WILL LET YOU DO ANYTHING, I WAS TOLD. A LANGUAGE THAT IS A PASSPORT, THAT WILL LET YOU GO ANYWHERE, BE ANYONE.
WHAT DID YOU WANT TO BE?
DO, NOT DID. AN ARTIST. MY MOTHER SAID I WAS BORN TO SING OR PLAY OR PAINT. BUT MY HEALTH WAS NOT GOOD. TOO FRAGILE.
AND YOU? WHAT IS IT YOU WANT, JUNO?
SOME PEOPLE AREN'T BORN FOR ANYTHING. CAN'T CHANGE WHO YOU ARE. CAN'T GET SOME STAINS OUT.
ALL I WANT IS TO ONE DAY NEVER TAKE ORDERS AGAIN. NOT FROM ANYONE.
BE CAREFUL, FATIMA--

THREE HOURS BEFORE.
"--THE WORLD ISN'T KIND TO FRAGILE THINGS."
TK
TKKA
TKKA
TKKA
TKKA
AH, FUCK. NO. JESUS, NO.
SR-3 VIKHR RIFLES. RUSSIAN MILITARY ISSUE. THESE DON'T COME CHEAP.
AH, FUCK!

EMILIO
A-KIÀ
DAVID, DAVID--ARE YOU HURT? DID HE GET YOU?
I'M FINE-- GO--
WHAT WAS HE DOING HERE?! HE'S A FUCKING KID, HE--
HE WAS ABOUT REBECCA'S AGE.
I'D WAGER HE WAS GUARDING THAT.

SEPTEMBER 1, 1993.
PROJECT DELTA CAME TO SOMALIA TO MAKE A BETTER WORLD.
DEFEND REFUGEES, DELIVER HUMANITARIAN AID, TRAIN TEACHERS AND MEDICS LOYAL TO AMERICAN CAUSES...
ما اسمك
FATIMA...
I SPEAK... SOME ENGLISH.
OCTOBER 3, 1993.
WE CAPTURED A PIRATED VESSEL OF MUNITIONS BEING SMUGGLED TO AIDID'S MEN. AIDID WAS THE SOMALIANS' TO KILL, BUT HE WAS OURS TO CRIPPLE.
I DON'T THINK JUNO EVER REALLY CARED ABOUT SOMALIA, OR AIDID, OR THE MISSION.
I DON'T EVEN THINK SHE REALLY CARED ABOUT ME.

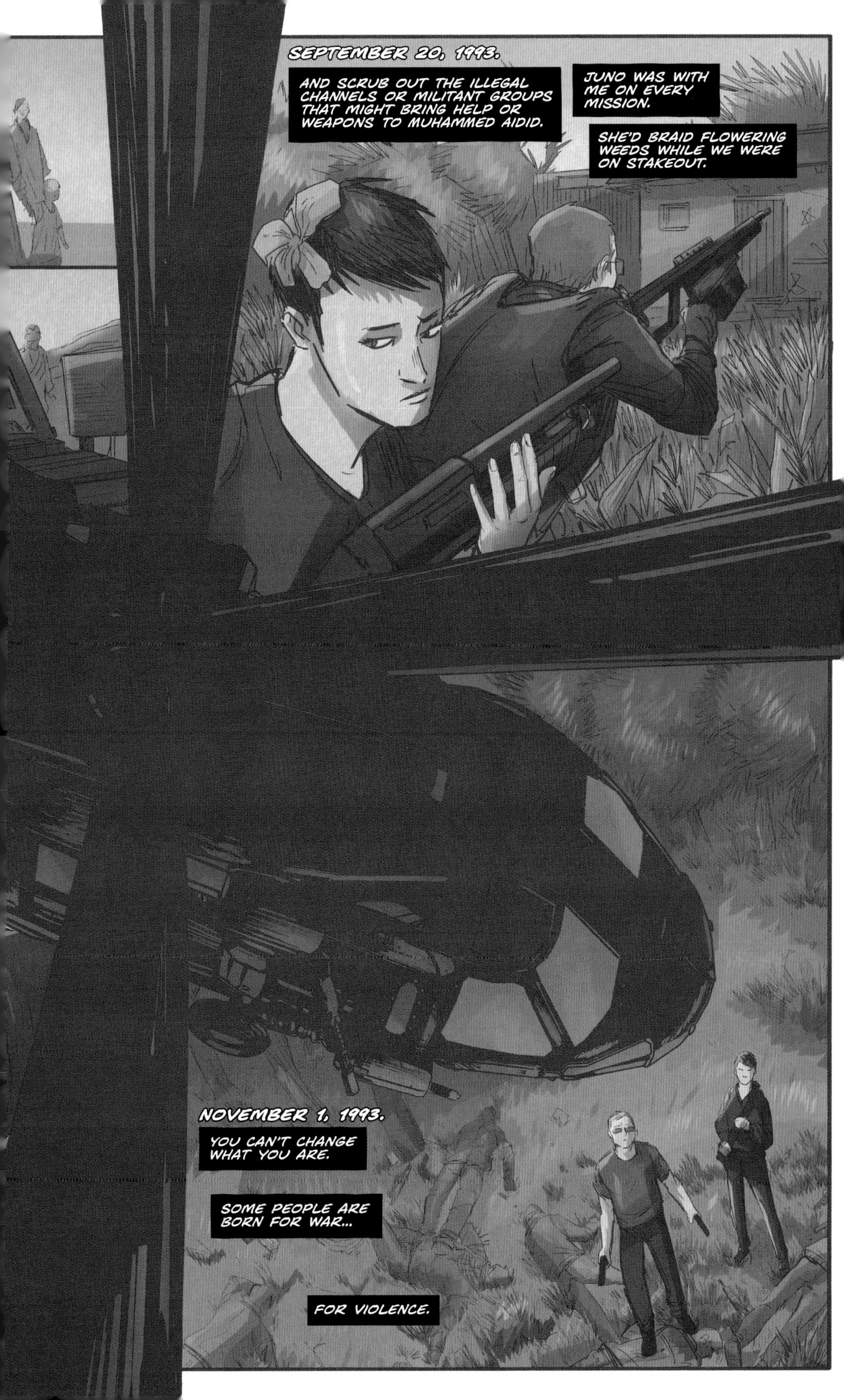
SEPTEMBER 20, 1993.
AND SCRUB OUT THE ILLEGAL CHANNELS OR MILITANT GROUPS THAT MIGHT BRING HELP OR WEAPONS TO MUHAMMED AIDID.
JUNO WAS WITH ME ON EVERY MISSION.
SHE'D BRAID FLOWERING WEEDS WHILE WE WERE ON STAKEOUT.
NOVEMBER 1, 1993.
YOU CAN'T CHANGE WHAT YOU ARE.
SOME PEOPLE ARE BORN FOR WAR...
FOR VIOLENCE.

AUGUST 21, 1993.
IN HEADLINES TODAY, THE UNITED NATIONS CALLS MOHAMMED AIDID A "WARLORD"--
--OF COURSE, AIDID RECEIVED MILITARY TRAINING IN THE FORMER SOVIET UNION AT THE FRUNZE MILITARY ACADEMY. A LOT OF PEOPLE FORGET THAT, TOM--
--THE SUBJECT OF A UNIFIED TASK FORCE, INCLUDING AMERICAN MILITARY PERSONNEL--

YOU DID IT, BOY! PRACTICAL INTEGRATION! PROJECT DELTA IS A GO!
THE OFFICIAL FOREIGN POLICY WAS THAT PROJECT DELTA WAS THERE IN A RELIEF EFFORT TO PROVIDE TRAINING AND HOUSING FOR SOMALI REFUGEES.
BUT IN THE END...IT WAS ONLY ABOUT MONEY.

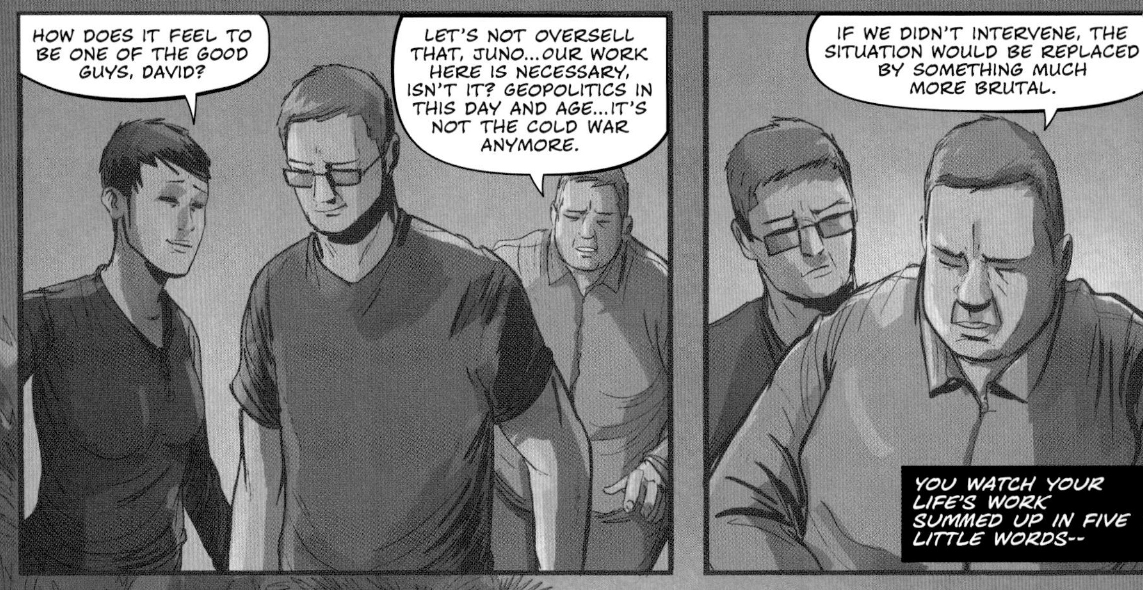
HOW DOES IT FEEL TO BE ONE OF THE GOOD GUYS, DAVID?
LET'S NOT OVERSELL THAT, JUNO...OUR WORK HERE IS NECESSARY, ISN'T IT? GEOPOLITICS IN THIS DAY AND AGE...IT'S NOT THE COLD WAR ANYMORE.
IF WE DIDN'T INTERVENE, THE SITUATION WOULD BE REPLACED BY SOMETHING MUCH MORE BRUTAL.
YOU WATCH YOUR LIFE'S WORK SUMMED UP IN FIVE LITTLE WORDS--
I SUPPOSE, DAVID...
THERE ARE NO GOOD GUYS.
--ISN'T HINDSIGHT A BITCH.

CHAPTER **FOUR**

ALEXANDRIA, VIRGINIA. NOW.
Taylor

WASHINGTON, DC. NOW.

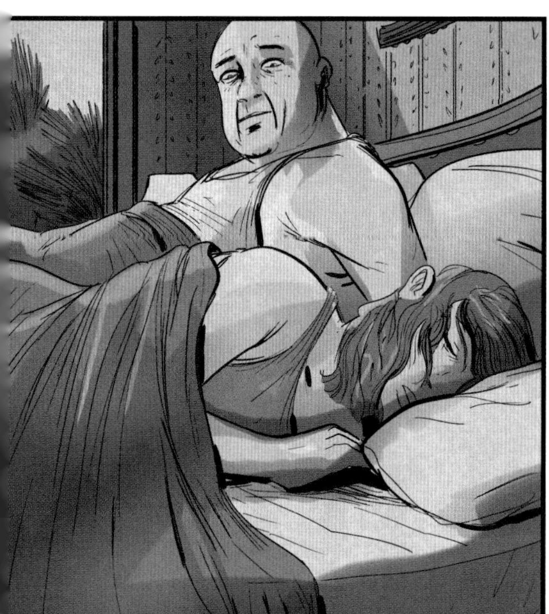

DON'T WORRY, PET! I'LL MAKE SURE THE KIDDOS ARE UP.

THERE'S A CAR WAITING FOR YOU DOWNSTAIRS. I DON'T WANT YOU HERE WHEN I COME HOME.

HOW'S M'BOY THIS MORNING? THAT YALE SWEATSHIRT ARRIVE YET?
HAHA, NOT YET. CAN'T YOU GET SOME CIA BUDDIES TO TRACK THE ORDER?
OH, SON, THE STORIES I COULD TELL.

I'LL SEE YOU TONIGHT, GIRLS! START THINKING ABOUT WHAT MOVIE YOU WANT TO SEE.

JUNO LUND

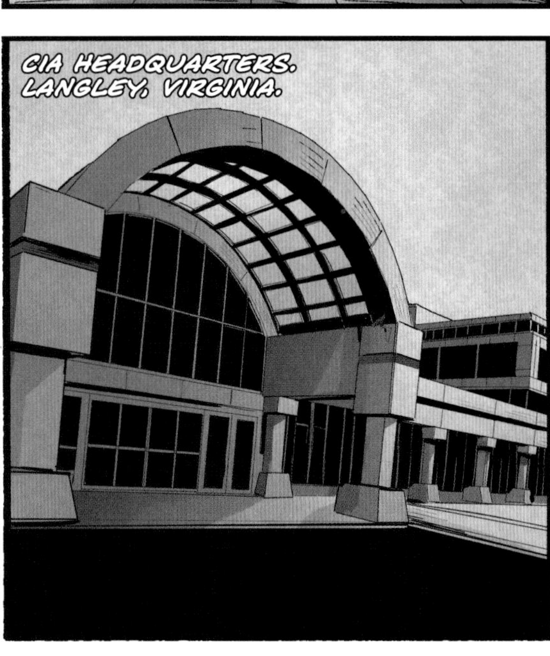
CIA HEADQUARTERS. LANGLEY, VIRGINIA.

THE PENTAGON, DEPARTMENT OF DEFENSE. WASHINGTON, DC.

MORNIN', BRUCE--

GOOD MORNING, JUNO. I WAS WONDERING IF YOU'D HEARD THE NEWS...
BARNEY TUTTLE. DEPUTY-DIRECTOR, SPECIAL OPERATIONS GROUP, CENTRAL INTELLIGENCE AGENCY.

NO, BARNEY, I HADN'T...
JUNO LUND. DIRECTOR OF HUMAN INTELLIGENCE, DEFENSE INTELLIGENCE AGENCY.

WHERE IS BUTTERFLY?

UE CORBEAU, VAL-DE-GRÂCE, PARIS.
I THREW THE OPERATIVE'S BODY FROM THE TRAIN. IT'S LOST OFF A GORGE IN THE MOUNTAINS IN...SOMEWHERE.
I WENT BACK TO THE SCENE OF THE SHOOTOUT.
THERE WERE NO POLICE. THERE WAS NO SIGN OF VIOLENCE AT ALL.
AND NIGHTINGALE--MY FATHER--WAS GONE.

BUT BEFORE I LEFT THE VINEYARD WHERE HE LIVED WITH HIS NEW FAMILY, HIS NEW CHILD...
HIS WIFE... ANGELIQUE GAVE ME SOMETHING.
SHE KNEW, SOMEHOW, I'D LOSE HIM.
DAD.
...REBECCA.
AND SHE KNEW I WOULD WANT TO COME BACK AGAIN.
"REVIENS."

WHAT YOU SAID ON THE ROAD, AFTER THE SHOOTOUT...
I COULD APOLOGIZE FOR LEAVING YOU. BUT I WON'T.
WE'RE ALL THE OTHER HAS RIGHT NOW.
BEFORE WE LEFT, ANGELIQUE GAVE ME A LIST--EMERGENCY CELL NUMBERS, ONLY TO BE USED IN THE WORST EMERGENCIES. ONE LED ME TO YOU.

I'VE BEEN CALLING ANGELIQUE AND MARTIN... THEY CHECKED IN THIS MORNING. BUT NOW...NO ANSWER.
WE'LL...NEED BRIDGEWELL LTD.
WHAT IS BRIDGEWELL LTD?
BRIDGEWELL... IS WHERE I WORK AS A... PRIVATE CONTRACTOR.

A MERCENARY? WE CAN'T TRUST A PACK OF MERCENARIES, WE'D JUST BE TRADING THE PROJECT FOR SOME OTHER--
BRIDGEWELL IS A VERY DISCERNING ORGANIZATION THAT HELPS PEOPLE LIKE US. GIVES US RESOURCES. THE PRIVATE SECTOR, REBECCA.

SO, *A MERCENARY.*
ONCE WE HAVE ANGELIQUE AND MARTIN, WE'LL NEED TO GO INTO HIDING.
OUTSIDE OF FICTION, LIFE ON THE RUN IS GRUELING, ISOLATING, AND EXCEPTIONALLY *EXPENSIVE*. WE COULD BE AT THIS FOR WEEKS, MONTHS, REBECCA.
I'VE BEEN HERE BEFORE.

I'LL SET UP A MEETING WITH A BRIDGEWELL GO-BETWEEN. THEY'LL GET US INFORMATION--
ON THE PROJECT, ON INTERPOL, ON WHO, WHY, AND HOW MIKHAIL ILCHENKO WAS KILLED.
THEY'LL PROTECT MY FAMILY.
WHO YOU'RE BRINGING ALONG THIS TIME, I NOTICED.

IF WE--YOU, ANGELIQUE, MARTIN, AND I--ARE GOING TO SURVIVE, WE NEED MONEY.
TO GET MONEY, THIS IS WHAT WE DO...AND THAT BUYS US *TIME AND FRIENDS.*
I...I HAVE AN IDEA. I THOUGHT ABOUT TRYING TO FIND MORTIMER OR HUXLEY THIS WAY--MY HANDLERS--

THIS IS THE AMOUNT OF DATA, TEXTS, AND PHONE CALLS USED ON THE THREE PHONES YOU GAVE ANGELIQUE, MARTIN, AND LEO.
SEE, THIS, HERE IS...AVERAGE. ONE HIGHER THAN OTHERS, PROBABLY PLAYING GAMES ON A CELL PHONE, THINGS LIKE THAT.
BUT THEN A FEW HOURS AGO...EVERYTHING FLATLINES.
MARTIN.

"NO INTERNET USE. NO INCOMING OR OUTGOING CALLS, EXCEPT FOR YOUR NUMBER. NOTHING."
"WE NEED TO GET TO THE SAFE HOUSE WHERE YOU SENT THEM. THEY'RE IN TROUBLE."

I CAN HEAR VOICES UPSTAIRS. RUSSIAN, ANGRY...
THIS WORLD OF CHAOS IS WHAT MY FATHER TOLD ME HE CALLS THE THEATER--
DONC, DESOLÉE! C'EST ANGELIQUE.

A MURKY SUBCULTURE WHERE CORPORATE AND POLITICAL INTERESTS COLLIDE.
JE NE SUIS PAS ICI EN CE MOMENT.

GOVERNMENT INSTITUTIONS, SECRET INTELLIGENCE BUREAUS, PRIVATE MERCENARY CONTRACTORS, ORGANIZED CRIME--
S'IL VOUS PLAÎT--

TRAFFICKING DRUGS, GUNS, HUMAN BEINGS--TERRORISM AND NUCLEAR PROLIFERATION--AND CONSTANT SURVEILLANCE.
--LAISSEZ-MOI UN MESSAGE DOUX--

I'M EXPECTING THE PROJECT. I'M EXPECTING AGENTS.
--ET JE REVIENS BIENTÔT!

NOT THIS.
CRASSSH

ILCHENKO'S MEN.
RUSSIAN MOB.

HOW DID YOU FIND US?
ПОЖАЛУЙСТА, ГОСПОЖА!
YOU'RE ONE OF ILCHENKO'S MEN. I HAD NOTHING TO DO WITH HIS MURDER.
PLEASE! LET ME LIVE--
TELL ME, AND I'LL CONSIDER IT...
WE--WE GO TO MOUNTAINS, AT FARM! WE SEE CAR LEAVE, DRIVEN BY MAN, WITH WOMAN INSIDE...
NO...
WE THINK THEY MURDERER AND BOSS...WE FOLLOW THEM TO PARIS...

WHAT I SAW, NO ONE SHOULD EVER SEE.
BUT I FELT NOTHING...ONLY A NAGGING SENSE OF INEVITABILITY.
THEY'RE NOT HERE. WE SHOULD GO.

DAD--!
BUT HE ALWAYS KNEW BETTER. ALWAYS.

THERE WAS A TIME, I THINK, THAT MY FATHER WOULD'VE INTERROGATED THIS MAN. TORTURED HIM.

NOT ANYMORE.

SOME STAINS NEVER WASH OUT.
YOU CAN'T RUN FROM WHO YOU ARE.

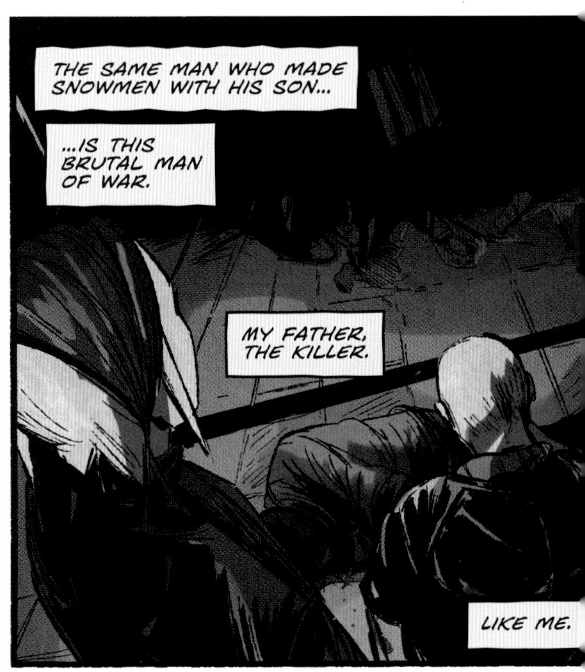
THE SAME MAN WHO MADE SNOWMEN WITH HIS SON...
...IS THIS BRUTAL MAN OF WAR.
MY FATHER, THE KILLER.
LIKE ME.

ANGELIQUE, SHE...SHE TOLD ME TO FIND THEM. MARTIN...THREE DAYS AGO, THEY WERE--
--SHE DIDN'T HAVE HER RING, WHY DID SHE GIVE ME HER RING-- MARTIN--

--WE HAVE TO BURY THEM, WE CAN'T JUST...
WE CAN'T BURY THEM. NO ONE CAN KNOW WE WERE HERE.
HOW MANY... HOW MANY WOMEN AND CHILDREN...

IF YOU HADN'T LEFT ME FOR DEAD IN THE MOUNTAINS, I'D HAVE BEEN HERE IN TIME...THEY'D HAVE STILL BEEN ALIVE.

HE DOESN'T SAY IT TO HURT ME.
THE POLICE ARE NEARLY HERE...
HE SAYS IT ONLY BECAUSE IT'S TRUE.
WE HAVE TO GO.

BUT THERE IS NOWHERE TO GO.
CAN... BRIDGEWELL HELP US?
CAN THEY GET US OUT OF THIS?
YES.

NEED THE...HÔPITAL DAPHNE...
BRIDGEWELL HAS A DOCTOR ON PAYROLL...
L'HÔPITAL DAPHNE, PARIS.
"YOU'D BE DEAD IN A WEEK," MY FATHER TOLD ME.
LIKE ANGELIQUE AND LEO. LIKE MARTIN.
HOPITAL DAPHNE
YOU'RE GOING TO BE FINE, DMITRI... BUT YOU CANNOT STAY HERE LONG.
WE NEED **PROTECTION**, AND **MONEY**, AND **ALLIES**...
AND--THOUGH HE DOES NOT SAY IT--REVENGE.
MY FATHER WAS TOO DRUGGED TO PLACE THE CALL.
EVER THE COMPANY MAN...TRADING ONE MASTER FOR ANOTHER.

I KEEP THINKING ABOUT THE BABY I ABANDONED IN THE HOTEL...AND ABOUT MARTIN, AND HIS DINOSAURS.
CLIK BRIDGEWELL LTD.
I DON'T FEEL LIKE A CHILD ANYMORE.

NIGHTINGALE ASKED ME TO CALL.
PASSWORD, PLEASE.
BRIDGEWELL: NOVEMBER ECHO VICTOR ALPHA ROMEO.

"WE NEED YOU TO TAKE US IN."
I AM A COLLECTION OF SKILLS.
KILLER, SPY, AND ACTRESS...
WELCOME TO THE THEATER.

ALEXANDRIA, VIRGINIA.
BUTTERFLY IS GONE.
ANY WORD?
NONE. OUR BEST AGENT.
YOU SEND ANYONE AFTER HER?
NO. SHE NEVER EVEN CALLED FOR EXTRACTION. NOT ONCE.
I CHECKED SATELLITE POSITIONING. SHE VANISHED THE MOMENT SHE SET FOOT IN OSLO.
I THOUGHT DEEP COVER... BUT SHE WOULD NEVER GO SO LONG.
NO. NOT BUTTERFLY.
DO YOU THINK SHE WAS KIDNAPPED? KILLED?
COMPROMISED, THEN?
JUNO...DO YOU THINK NIGHTINGALE MIGHT BE ALIVE?

AUGUST, 1993.
I WANTED TO MAKE A BETTER WORLD.
I CALLED IT PROJECT DELTA--
THE PROJECT.

1988. FIVE YEARS BEFORE THE START OF PROJECT DELTA.
IT FELT MORE LIKE A BOARD MEETING THAN A MILITARY OPERATION. BUT I COULDN'T AFFORD TO BE IDEOLOGICAL. GOOD SOLDIERS SELDOM CAN.
--A SHIFTING PROGRAM OF INDEPENDENT SPYING UNITS THAT CAN BLEN INTO COUNTRIES WHER NO AMERICAN PRESENC HAS EVER BEEN AUTHORIZED.

WE'LL LOSE THEM FOR MONTHS AT A TIME. THEY CAN BE ANYONE, ANYWHERE, AND ALTER THEIR APPEARANCES, LANGUAGE, DIALECT, ENTIRE HISTORY--
--AS UNRECOGNIZABLE FROM ONE INCARNATION TO THE NEXT, AS A CATERPILLAR TO A BUTTERFLY.

THIS WILL BE PRACTICAL INTEGRATION AT WORK.
WE ARRIVE, QUELL HOSTILITIES, OFFER SUPPLIES THROUGH THE REGION, AND INDOCTRINATE LOCALS WITH TRAINING RELEVANT TO THEIR CRISIS.
STABLE, GRATEFUL COUNTRIES ARE IN EVERYBODY'S BEST INTERESTS. THEY'RE GOOD FOR BUSINESS, GOOD FOR GLOBAL SECURITY, AND GOOD, ABOVE ALL ELSE, FOR US.
BARI
GALGUDUUD

WHO WOULDN'T WANT STABLE COUNTRIES?
CORPORATIONS THAT BENEFIT FROM WAR, IT TURNS OUT.

THESE NEW OPERATIVES AREN'T AGENTS; THEY AREN'T MEANT TO KILL. THEY'RE ACTORS, FOR ESPIONAGE ONLY.
DEPARTMENT OF DEFENSE
UNITED STATES OF AMERICA

PROJECT DELTA EMBRACES THE IDEA THAT WAR WILL NO LONGER BE FOUGHT ACROSS DIRECT NATIONAL LINES.
WE ANTICIPATE NEW TECHNOLOGIES
IF *THEY* ARE EVERYWHERE, THEN ***WE*** MUST BE EVERYWHERE. THAT IS WHAT MAKES PROJECT DELTA UNIQUE.

OUR AGENTS WILL INFILTRATE THE FABRIC OF THESE SOCIETIES, AND INTO THE HEART OF OUR ENEMIES' INFRASTRUCTURE.
THEY WILL DISRUPT ANYTHING THAT IS NOT IN OUR INTERESTS OR IN THE INTERESTS OF THE PEACE-LOVING PEOPLE OF THESE COUNTRIES.
WE WILL HELP TO FOSTER BETTER EDUCATION, A BETTER ECONOMY FOR THESE NATIONS...BUT OUR PURPOSE IS NOT PURELY ALTRUISTIC.

AT THE TIME, I DIDN'T FULLY TRUST THE INTENTIONS OF EITHER THE CIA OR THE DEPARTMENT OF DEFENSE. EACH WANTED CONTROL OF A MISSION THEY'D LAUGHED AT A YEAR AGO.
AT THE TIME, I'D BEEN HAPPY THAT WE HAD FUNDING.
I WAS MAKING A SAFER WORLD FOR MY DAUGHTER.
IN THE COMING MONTHS, I'D REALIZE THEIR CONFLICTS OF INTEREST HAD NOTHING TO DO WITH NATIONAL SECURITY...AND A LOT MORE TO DO WITH WHOSE WALLET GOT THICKER.

I HAD SEEN THE WORLD. I KNEW WHAT IT NEEDED.
I'D SEEN HAITI IN '87.
NICARAGUA IN '85.
HONDURAS IN '84, AND ON.

IRAN IN '86.
I THOUGHT I KNEW WHAT THE WORLD NEEDED.
I WAS JUST ONE MORE IDEALIST PRETENDING HE WOULDN'T BE A TYRANT, IF HE COULD.

WINCHESTER, VIRGINIA. 1988
MIRANDA POWELL. DEPUTY SECRETARY OF DEFENSE.
SHOULDN'T YOU TAKE THE RIFLE AWAY FROM HER?
THE SAFETY IS ON. SHE GETS UNHOLY-ANGRY WHEN YOU TAKE THE RIFLE AWAY FROM HER.
AH.

ADMITTEDLY, THERE HAS BEEN SOME INTERNAL CONFLICT REGARDING WHO WILL COMMAND PROJECT DELTA, AND YOU.
THE CIA IS NOT HAPPY TO LOSE YOU TO THE DEPARTMENT OF DEFENSE.

TO WHAT DO I OWE THE PLEASURE? I CAN'T IMAGINE A SOCIAL CALL BRINGS THE LIKES OF MIRANDA POWELL ALL THE WAY OUT TO MY QUIET VIRGINIA FARMHOUSE.
SENIOR PENTAGON HAS INTERNS FOR THAT, I'M SURE.
I BRING GOOD NEWS, MR. FAULKNER.
THE DEPARTMENT OF DEFENSE IS VERY INTERESTED IN YOUR PROPOSITION FOR PROJECT DELTA.
THEY BELIEVE... **WE BELIEVE**...IT COULD BRING A GREAT DEAL OF GOOD TO THE WORLD.
NIGHTINGALES, AREN'T THEY? I THINK IT WOULD MAKE A LOVELY CODENAME FOR YOU, IF THE PROJECT PROGRESSES.
A SUBTLE GRAY BIRD, SINGING SUCH AN ***INTERESTING*** SONG.
AS WITH ANY TRULY NOBLE ENDEAVOR, MR. FAULKNER...YOU MAY DO SOME VERY UGLY THINGS IN THE NAME OF A BETTER WORLD.
I KNOW.

WINCHESTER, VIRGINIA. 1988.
TEN MINUTES BEFORE.
I PUT THE GUN INTO MY DAUGHTER'S HANDS.
AND I WATCHED THE PIECES FALL.
THE RED MIST, SO LIKE WINE, SO LIKE BLOOD.
CRKKK

AND WITH EVERY UGLY SCRAP OF STRENGTH INSIDE ME
I WISHED TO AN EMPTY HEAVEN

THAT REBECCA'S LIFE

WOULD NEVER BE LIKE MINE.
the end

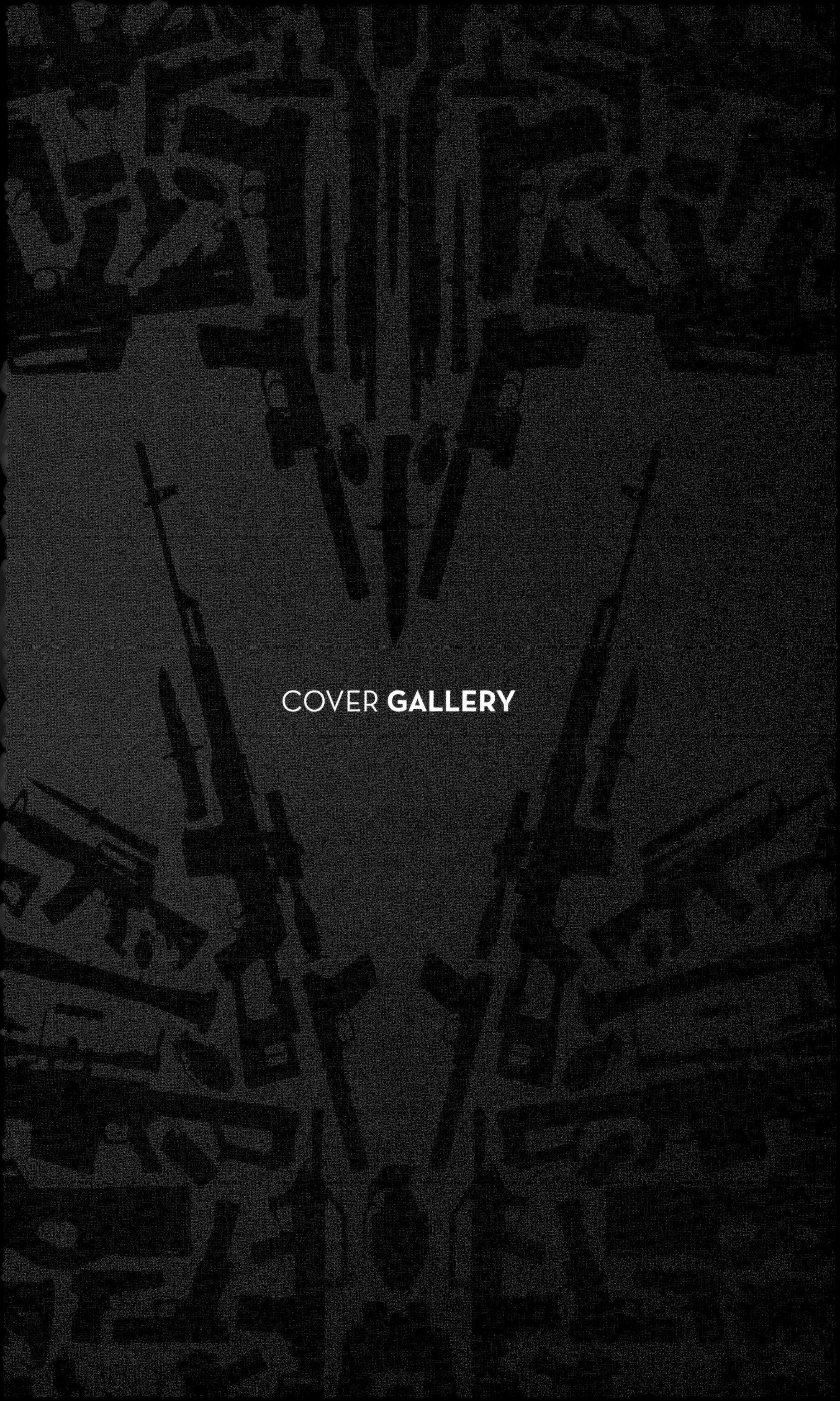

COVER **GALLERY**

ISSUE ONE COVER BY
PHIL **NOTO**
noto

ISSUE TWO COVER BY
PHIL NOTO

ISSUE THREE COVER BY
PHIL **NOTO**

ISSUE FOUR COVER BY
PHIL NOTO
noto

PIN UP BY
JAY **SHAW**

BEHIND THE SCENES

SCRIPT TO PAGE

ISSUE ONE, PAGE ONE

PANEL ONE: An establishing shot of Northern Virginia pines, in the stillness of the forest. It's about an hour until sunset, everything green and gold and shadowed.

LOCATOR CAPTION: Winchester, Virginia. 1988.

BUTTERFLY CAPTION: The wait.

PANEL TWO: A number of WINE BOTTLES rest on a rickety fence in front of the pines. (Regarding the construction of the label, the bottle reads "Le Papillon Rose" for its producing vineyard, "Beaujolais" for its region/wine type, and "1983"—it should also have a pink butterfly visible on the label.)

BUTTERFLY CAPTION: The aim.

PANEL THREE: One of the BOTTLES explodes, SHARDS raining in all directions. Here is the violence implicit in the lives of our characters, the red glass shards like blood.

SFX: CRKKKM

PANEL FOUR: A larger panel. DAVID FAULKNER is teaching his daughter REBECCA to shoot. REBECCA is about seven years old; she is holding the RIFLE, but her father is holding her. They are both peering, intent, at the mist of red glass in the air from the shattered WINE BOTTLE.

BUTTERFLY CAPTION: Before he passed, my father taught me to shoot.

PANEL FIVE: CLOSE on DAVID'S HAND around REBECCA'S on the trigger of the rifle.

BUTTERFLY CAPTION: He'd die gagging on his own blood later that year, somewhere in the Somali desert.

ISSUE ONE, PAGE TWO

PANEL ONE: REBECCA looks up at her FATHER. Her face is blank and impassive, completely trusting; her eyes are huge and blue, the pupils tight as pinpricks.

BUTTERFLY CAPTION: I don't know if this memory is real.

PANEL TWO: DAVID looks away from her, over her head, towards someone who has just arrived. He looks concerned.

BUTTERFLY CAPTION: Memory is so delicate, like the rest of us.

PANEL THREE: DAVID walks away, his hand indicating she is to sit tight. She is still holding the RIFLE.

BUTTERFLY CAPTION: The little things kill us, in the end.

PANEL FOUR: REBECCA has raised the RIFLE, aiming into the forest.

BUTTERFLY CAPTION: The kernel of plaque in the aorta.

PANEL FIVE: A little gray BIRD flies up out of the pines—a little nightingale.

BUTTERFLY CAPTION: The bead of blood in the fissure of the brain.

PANEL SIX: The BIRD explodes in a burst of blood, bone, and feather.

BUTTERFLY CAPTION: The tip of a brass coated .22 round at 890mph.

ISSUE TWO, PAGE EIGHT

PANEL ONE: BUTTERFLY hands NIGHTINGALE the bottle of wine.

BUTTERFLY: When I was a child, my father, David Faulkner, had this one wine…not even a good kind.

BUTTERFLY: This cheap, fruity stuff--I never knew why it was so…He saved it for special occasions.

PANEL TWO: NIGHTINGALE studies the label.

BUTTERFLY (off panel): What were you toasting, on that special day?

PANEL THREE: CLOSE on the wine label, and the LITTLE PINK BUTTERFLY on its logo.

BUTTERFLY (off panel): The day you…what? Faked your death?

PANEL FOUR: NIGHTINGALE looks up at her. His face is completely cool, not penitent,

not angry. He still doesn't want it to be true…and if it is true, he wants to drive her away for her own safety. BUTTERFLY'S expression is closed, but her blue eyes are bright and angry.

NIGHTINGALE: So?

BUTTERFLY: Why are you being so cruel?

PANEL FIVE: NIGHTINGALE'S expression is haunted, coming to terms with who she is and what he owes her. BUTTERFLY is conflicted, looking away from him.

NIGHTINGALE: If you had any idea how many women and children…

NIGHTINGALE: But you're a child.

BUTTERFLY: I'm two years older than your wife, who is far gentler and more forgiving than you could ever deserve.

ISSUE TWO, PAGE NINE

PANEL ONE: NIGHTINGALE reasserts control. His look is concerned now, more responsible—responsible for her, too—paternal.

NIGHTINGALE: Tell me how you got here. Tell me everything.

PANEL TWO: CLOSE on BUTTERFLY'S FACE, tense, watchful, but without outward signs of suspicion.

BUTTERFLY CAPTION: My Project…or my father?
BUTTERFLY CAPTION: What could I gain by telling him? Trust? Information?
BUTTERFLY CAPTION: The Project hasn't come for me…and he could be the key to why.

PANEL THREE: Some time has passed. NIGHTINGALE is studying the maps and travel guides she used, as BUTTERFLY points out her course. NIGHTINGALE'S face is dark and even a bit frightening.

BUTTERFLY: --then when I was on the hill overlooking the vineyard, I called the

third number again, the one I'd never tried before, for extraction--

NIGHTINGALE: No…

PANEL FOUR: NIGHTINGALE jumps up from his armchair, disturbing the OVERHEAD LAMP. The maps and travel guide fall to the floor.

NIGHTINGALE: Get up. We have to leave, now--

PANEL FIVE: NIGHTINGALE whirls on his DAUGHTER.

NIGHTINGALE: You amateur. You've led the Project and the rest right to us.

PANEL SIX: Tiny panel! Close on BUTTERFLY, echoing her father's contempt. Even just her eerie eyes, or her mouth.

BUTTERFLY: So?

ISSUE FOUR, PAGE TWENTY TWO

PANEL ONE: An establishing shot of Northern Virginia pines, in the stillness of the forest. It's about an hour until sunset, everything green and gold and shadowed.

LOCATOR CAPTION: Winchester, Virginia. 1988. Ten Minutes Before.

2 NIGHTINGALE CAPTION: I put the gun into my daughter's hands

PANEL TWO: A red clay pigeon TARGET flies up in front of the pines.

NIGHTINGALE CAPTION: and I watched the pieces fall.

PANEL THREE: The TARGET explodes in the air, SHARDS raining in all directions, the red dust like a burst of blood.

NIGHTINGALE CAPTION: The red mist, so like wine, so like blood

SFX: CRKKK!

PANEL FOUR: A larger panel. DAVID FAULKNER is teaching his daughter REBECCA to shoot. REBECCA is about seven years old; she is holding the RIFLE, but her father is holding her. They are both peering, intent, at the mist of red clay in the air from the shattered TARGET that Rebecca has just destroyed. This is almost the identical image from Issue #1.1.4, though inverted and facing a different direction.

NIGHTINGALE CAPTION: and with every ugly scrap of strength inside me

NIGHTINGALE CAPTION: I wished to an empty heaven

PANEL FIVE: NIGHTINGALE rises, his hand on his daughter's shoulder. She is still holding the rifle, peering up at him.

NIGHTINGALE CAPTION: that Rebecca's life

PANEL SIX: NIGHTINGALE walks to meet MIRANDA at the car.

NIGHTINGALE CAPTION: would never be like mine.

ABOUT THE **AUTHORS**

ARASH **AMEL** is screenwriter and producer who lives and works in Los Angeles. He has developed, and continues to work on, numerous film projects at major Hollywood studios, including Warner Brothers, Universal Pictures and Twentieth Century Fox. His previous feature credits include the spy thriller *The Expatriate*, starring Aaron Eckhart, and *Grace of Monaco*, which opened the Cannes Film Festival in 2014. When he's not writing, he's hanging out with his wife, son, dog and cat.

MARGUERITE **BENNETT** is a comic book writer from Richmond, Virginia who currently lives in New York City. She attended the Maggie L. Walker Governor's School and received her MFA in Creative Writing from Sarah Lawrence College in 2013. She has worked for DC Comics, Marvel, BOOM! Studios, and IDW on projects ranging from *Batman* and *A-Force* to Fox's *Sleepy Hollow*. She has been fortunate enough to see over a million copies of her work published.

ANTONIO **FUSO** is a comic book artist and illustrator known for his sharp and frenetic style. Works include the graphic novels *A Sickness in the Family* and *The Girl Who Played With Fire* (Vertigo) and *GI Joe: Cobra* (IDW). He lives and works in Rome, Italy, and is addicted to caffeine.

STEFANO **SIMEONE** is an illustrator and comic book artist who has collaborated with Red Bull, Image Comics, il Mucchio, XL di Repubblica, Sergio Bonelli Editore, Aurea Editoriale, IDW, Archaia, BOOM! Studios, and Verticalismi. His first book, *Semplice* (Tunué), won the Romics 2013 award for the Best Italian Book and the Boscarato 2013 award for Best New Author. In October 2013, Bao Publishing published his book *Ogni piccolo pezzo*, which won the Rimini the Smiting award for comics. Stefano is now working on his third graphic novel, which will come out in September 2015 from Bao Publishing. When he is not at the Skeleton Monster studio, he lives in the west wing of the Wayne mansion (which is in Rome, as everybody knows) with his girlfriend.

ADAM **GUZOWSKI** has always been an avid lover of the illustrative arts. After attending the Joe Kubert School, Adam began working as a freelance colorist and illustrator. His work has been published by many comic book publishers, including Archaia, BOOM! Studios, and Image Comics, among others.

STEVE **WANDS** is a Harvey Award-nominated letterer and all-round swell fellow. He leaves a trail of ABC's across the pages of many BOOM! Studios, DC, Image, and Kodansha Comics' titles and does some other stuff too (like illustrating, inking, coloring, writing, making peanut butter and jelly sammiches). Most notably he lives in New Jersey with his wife and sons. Oh, and he drinks a lot of coffee.